The Perfect Match

Leslie James

SCHOLASTIC INC.
New York Toronto London Auckland Sydney
Mexico City New Delhi Hong Kong Buenos Aires

**Cover photo
James Levin**

**Illustrations
Melissa Salyers**

3   4   5   6   7   8   9   10   23   10   09   08   07   06   05   04   03

Contents

Contents

Kirsten Starsia had been stretching for ten minutes. She looked at her watch. The school newspaper reporter was twenty minutes late. *Where could he be?*

She looked around the practice field. But there was no sign of anyone. Kirsten sighed. She had tons of homework. She was tired and sweaty from soccer practice. She just wanted to go home and take a shower.

She sat down on the bleachers. She really wanted the soccer team to be in the paper. So she decided to wait for five more minutes.

Then Kirsten saw a tall guy in the distance. He was jogging toward her. "Finally," she said out loud. His legs looked a little too long for him. And he kind of stumbled as he ran. But Kirsten thought there was something cute about him.

She stood up to say hello. But before she could get a word out, Jeff Kinsel fell to the ground. His notebook flew out of his arms. Papers went everywhere. Somehow, he had tripped over his own feet.

"You've got to be kidding me," Kirsten said to herself.

Jeff heard her. *Great,* he thought, *this is going to go well.*

Jeff was editor-in-chief of the school paper. He usually didn't cover sports. And that was fine with him. He didn't know anything about sports, and he didn't care. But Tom, the sports reporter, was home with mono. So Jeff had to cover for him.

Jeff started to pick up his papers. They kept flying around. He felt as if he were running in circles. *She could at least help me,* thought Jeff. *Why are so many jocks snobs?*

"Are you Kristen?" he asked as he reached for the last paper.

"It's *Kirsten.* And yes, of course I am. Do you see anyone else out here?"

"I guess not," said Jeff. He started to put his

notes in order. *What's up with her?*

Kirsten watched Jeff look at his papers. Then she lost her patience. "Are we going to start this thing?" *And how about saying you're sorry for being late?*

Kirsten was mad. Soccer was a new sport for her school. And the team really needed people to get behind them. It was great the school paper wanted to do the story. But who *was* this clueless guy they had sent?

She stared at Jeff. He stared back. He tried not to look away. He told himself he shouldn't care. But he hated looking bad in front of girls like Kristen. Or Kirsten, or whatever it was. He'd noticed her before in the lunch room. She was athletic and very cute. She hung out with all the popular girls. Most of them thought they were too cool to speak to normal human beings. But she had seemed different. She seemed almost, well, nice.

He must have been wrong.

"So, do you want me to tell you about the team?" Kirsten asked.

"What team do you play on again?" he

smirked.

"The soccer team!"

He thought she was going to hit him. *Does she have any sense of humor?*

"Just kidding," he said. But he still had no idea where his notes were. He decided he'd try to fake it.

"So, they tell me you're a halfback," he guessed.

"No, I play center forward," corrected Kirsten.

"Okay, of course," said Jeff. He was usually prepared. But this time he wasn't. He wondered what the positions meant, anyway.

"And as center forward, your job is to . . . ?" Jeff waited for Kirsten to fill in the blank.

Is he serious? Kirsten wondered. "I make all the goals. And I stop the other team from scoring. I teach the rest of the team how to play. I schedule our games. Oh, and I pack the team snacks."

"What kind of snacks?" asked Jeff.

"I'm kidding!" Kirsten said. *What an idiot,* she thought.

"I know," Jeff said quickly. But he hadn't been sure.

Kirsten took a deep breath. "Okay, my main job is to score," she said. "But other players do that too. And we have a great goalie. That's the person who guards the goal. Get it? *Goal*-ie."

Jeff knew she was making fun of him. But he couldn't think of anything to say. So he just stared at her. She stared back, waiting for another question. Jeff just wanted the interview to be over.

Kirsten decided to plow ahead. "Well, so far this year, we've played five games. We're totally undefeated. In two weeks, we play the Tigers. They're our biggest rivals. It's a home game. So it would be fantastic if we could get the whole school out for that game. Because if we win . . ."

Then Kirsten stopped. She couldn't believe it. Jeff was looking at his watch. "Am I keeping you?" she asked.

"Yeah, but don't worry about it," said Jeff.

"I won't," said Kirsten. Now she was really mad.

Jeff laughed. "I was just kidding," he said.

Kirsten made herself smile.

Five minutes later, they had run out of things to talk about.

"Okay, I think I have all I need. Thanks, Kristen." Jeff got up quickly.

"It's *Kir*-sten."

"Right. I'll talk to you later," Jeff said. He turned around and walked back to the newspaper office. *Man, she's impossible! And I have no idea what I'm going to write about.*

Kirsten gathered her gear. She walked to the locker room. "What a loser," she said out loud. She threw her stuff in her locker and headed home.

Jeff walked back to the newspaper office. With every step he thought of another question he should have asked. He felt embarrassed. Then he felt mad. *How rude was that girl? And who did she think she was, anyway?*

The office was empty, except for Isabelle, the arts editor. Jeff threw his stuff on his desk. "I just interviewed the Soccer Queen of Cleveland High," he said. "I totally blew it, too. When is Tom coming back? I'm sick of all this extra work."

Isabelle laughed. "I don't know. And guess what? I have another story for you." She waved a piece of paper at Jeff.

"What?" asked Jeff. He sat down next to Isabelle. He loved talking to her. She was from Paris. She had black hair and steel-blue eyes.

And Jeff could listen to her accent all day. He loved the way she pronounced her th's like z's. And she always called him "Zheff."

Jeff thought Isabelle was the best thing about the newspaper. She listened to the best new bands. She always had tickets to the hottest shows. And she knew about cool movies before anyone else. Thanks to Isabelle, the arts section was the most popular part of the paper.

"You won't believe it," she said. "The student council is putting personal ads on the school Web site. You find the perfect match. Then you meet them at the Valentine's Day dance. *Voilà!*" She smirked and tossed the flyer at Jeff.

Jeff groaned. "Valentine's Day is so lame. It was only invented so greeting card companies could make money. It's so corny."

"That's so romantic," Isabelle said with a smirk. "Now we know why you don't have a girlfriend."

"Oh, give me a break," Jeff said, feeling a little hurt.

"Sorry," said Isabelle. Then she pointed at Jeff. "I think you should write something about the site. Look at it tonight. Maybe you will get in the mood."

"Right," sighed Jeff. He shoved the flyer into his backpack.

"Come on, Zheff. Who knows? Maybe you will meet your perfect match. And me, too. I do not have a date for the dance. Maybe I will find a nice American guy." She winked at Jeff and then left the office.

❤ ❤ ❤ ❤

Kirsten was walking home. She was really tired. Practice had been long. Then she had to wait for that stupid reporter. And for what?

"Hey, Kirsten, want a ride?" She looked up to see Mike. He was leaning out of his blue sports car. His football shirt was wet with sweat from practice.

"Am *I* glad to see *you*," Kirsten said. She got into the car.

"What's going on?" asked Mike.

"I just gave an interview to the school paper," Kirsten said. "The reporter didn't know a thing about soccer. I know he's going to mess everything up."

"How bad could it be?" asked Mike. "As long as everyone comes out for the Tigers game."

Kirsten smiled. Mike was such a great friend. He was the best receiver on the football team. But he still showed up for her games. He even missed a practice for one.

In the off-season, they hung out a lot after school. They'd go shoot baskets sometimes. Or they'd go to the movies.

Sometimes Kirsten wished they talked more about important stuff. But she always felt comfortable around Mike. Plus, he had the most gorgeous eyes she had ever seen.

"You hear about this Internet dating thing?" Mike asked.

"Yeah," she said. "Sounds stupid to me."

"What's so bad about it?"

"I don't know," Kirsten said. "Those kind of things never work out. And Valentine's Day is stupid anyway."

Mike didn't say a word. Kirsten thought his face fell. He looked almost hurt.

"So, are you going to the dance?" she asked.

"I dunno, maybe," he said. Then he changed the subject. "Hey, I have to get some gas. Do you mind coming along?"

"Nope," said Kirsten.

"Kirsten, pick up the phone!" yelled Mrs. Starsia.

"Hello!" Kirsten said as she sank into the pillows on her bed.

"Hey, it's Steph."

"What's up?" asked Kirsten. She had hoped it would be Mike.

"You're never going to believe this," Steph said.

"Believe what?" Kirsten played along. Steph was always calling about something that Kirsten was "never going to believe."

"Okay, are you ready?"

"I'm ready, already! Come on, tell me!" Kirsten was getting impatient.

"Okay. I, Stephanie Jean Garrison . . . I can't believe I did this . . ."

"Steph, if you don't tell me right now, I am going to hang up!"

"Okay, okay. I just put a personal ad on the student council's Web site." She blurted it out in one breath. Then she giggled into the phone. "I felt totally lame. But then I was like, hey, it's just for fun. And then I thought maybe something *good* will happen. I don't know. It's worth a shot. Right?"

"Are you serious?" asked Kirsten. "I mean, yeah, of course you're right. It's no big deal or anything. I just can't believe you actually did it!" She walked to her desk and called up the Web site. "Actually, it looks like lots of people have put ads up."

"Why don't you do it too?" Steph said.

"Me?" Kirsten said, trying to sound casual. She looked around the site.

"Or you could just keep drooling over your buddy Mike," said Steph. "You are so in love with him—admit it!"

"Cut it out," said Kirsten. "You know he's just a friend."

"Oh, here we go. *Just a friend*," Steph mocked. "Whatever. Spare me. Just fill out a form, and call me later."

Kirsten hung up. She started cleaning up her room. But a few minutes later, she found herself back at the computer. *No one has to know,* she thought. And she found the "Perfect Match" Web site.

```
┌─────────────────────────────────────────────┐
│ ▀▀▀▀▀▀▀▀▀▀ PerfectMatch ▀▀▀▀▀▀▀▀▀ ⊡⊟ │
│                                               │
│     PERFECT                                   │
│            Match ♡♡                           │
│                                               │
│  ┌─────────┬──────────────┬──────────────┬───────────┐ │
│  │ Welcome │ All About You...│ Your Ideal Match│Tell a Friend│ │
│  └─────────┴──────────────┴──────────────┴───────────┘ │
│  Favorite book: |                             │
│  Favorite movie:                              │
│  Favorite food:                               │
│  Favorite TV show:                            │
│  My best date:                                │
│  My worst date:                               │
│  My ideal match:                              │
│  Myself:                                      │
│        Click here to search for your ideal match. │
│                                               │
│    All correspondence is as anonymous as you choose. │
│   If you make a "love connection," you can meet your match │
│      at the Valentine's Day dance. Happy searching! │
│                                               │
└─────────────────────────────────────────────┘
```

18

Kirsten smiled. "This is so stupid," she said. Then she started writing her profile.

🖤 🖤 🖤 🖤

Jeff finished his lab report. He closed his book. Then he logged onto the Internet. He hated to admit it, but he was curious about the "Perfect Match" Web site. He told himself that he was just doing research for the article. Then he started looking for interesting profiles.

"Etoile" caught his eye. *"Etoile," French for star. Hmmm. Couldn't be Isabelle, could it?*

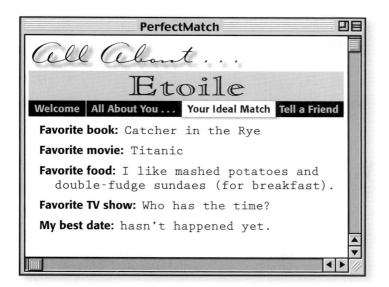

PerfectMatch

All About . . .

Etoile

| Welcome | All About You . . . | Your Ideal Match | Tell a Friend |

Favorite book: Catcher in the Rye

Favorite movie: Titanic

Favorite food: I like mashed potatoes and double-fudge sundaes (for breakfast).

Favorite TV show: Who has the time?

My best date: hasn't happened yet.

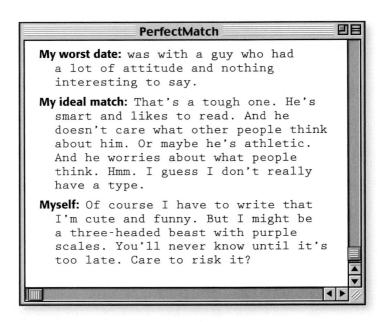

PerfectMatch

My worst date: was with a guy who had a lot of attitude and nothing interesting to say.

My ideal match: That's a tough one. He's smart and likes to read. And he doesn't care what other people think about him. Or maybe he's athletic. And he worries about what people think. Hmm. I guess I don't really have a type.

Myself: Of course I have to write that I'm cute and funny. But I might be a three-headed beast with purple scales. You'll never know until it's too late. Care to risk it?

Jeff smiled. He wrote his own profile. Then he emailed "Etoile."

I was surfing the site and saw your profile. I think we're perfect for each other. I'm a book-loving geek on weekdays. Then on Friday night, I turn into a muscle-bound football star. My friends think I'm crazy. But it sounds like you'll understand me. Oh, and I have purple scales. Just one question, What's up with TITANIC? That movie sounds too corny for you.

Madscribbler

♥ ♥ ♥ ♥

Seconds later, Kirsten's inbox bleeped. She clicked on her mailbox and saw that she had a message from someone named "Madscribbler."

She read his profile.

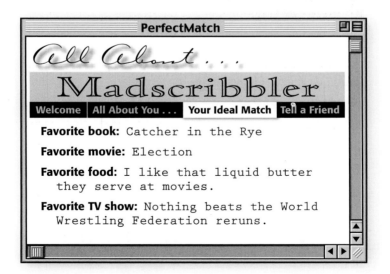

PerfectMatch

All About . . .

Madscribbler

| Welcome | All About You . . . | **Your Ideal Match** | Tell a Friend |

Favorite book: Catcher in the Rye

Favorite movie: Election

Favorite food: I like that liquid butter they serve at movies.

Favorite TV show: Nothing beats the World Wrestling Federation reruns.

My best date: was in fifth grade. This girl named Stacey asked me to help her sell lemonade on Saturday afternoon. She was my big crush. I was so nervous. I gave everyone the wrong change. That was impressive. Why? The lemonade cost 25 cents a cup, and most people paid with a quarter! Stacey fired me after I spilled lemonade on a customer.

My worst date: was a year ago when I went on a real date with Stacey! Finally, I had a chance to show her the real me. Yeah, right.

My car ran out of gas right after I picked her up. No joke. And then I realized that I had forgotten my wallet.

Stacey had to help me push my car to the gas station. Then she had to loan me money for gas. Then she made me take her home. My only lucky break? She moved a few weeks later.

My ideal match: is someone who can laugh while pushing a car.

Myself: Forget what Stacey thinks. I am the perfect guy.

Kirsten laughed and emailed him back. She wondered if Madscribbler was Mike. He wasn't usually that funny. But the name "Madscribbler" would make sense. Mike was always drawing comics. He plays football. And he *did* seem pretty aware of his gas tank the other day.

Hey, Madscribbler. You definitely know books. But I'm worried about your taste in movies. I mean, TITANIC has everything—romance, drama, suspense. Okay, maybe it is sort of corny. But you can't tell me you didn't cry at the end! By the way, have you ever tried popcorn butter on mashed potatoes?
Etoile

Etoile: Popcorn butter goes well with anything. As for TITANIC, I don't know.... You probably just like watching the wind in Leo's hair. I guess I have to admit that it was pretty entertaining. But I'm not commenting on the crying thing.
Madscribbler

Leo's not bad, as movie stars go. Whatever. So, what year are you?
Etoile

I'm a senior. Almost out of here. And you, Ms. Star?
Madscribbler

I'm a senior, too. I see the "étoile" thing didn't fool you.
Etoile

Well, I am quite sophisticated. Couldn't you tell?
Madscribbler

Sure, your taste in TV shows gave you away.
Etoile

I knew that would help me find a good match.

So, your worst date had lots of attitude and nothing interesting to say. It's funny how you can have an image of someone. Then they end up being nothing like that. I mean, I really thought Stacey was cool. But it turned out she was mean and not much fun. You'd think I would have figured that out back in fifth grade!

Madscribbler

Hey, I'd fire you for spilling lemonade too. :) But I know what you mean about having images of people. I don't know which are harder to shake— good impressions or bad ones.

Etoile

4

Jeff yawned during first period English class. He had spent almost all night emailing "Etoile." Now, he was having a hard time staying awake. Last night's emails kept running through his head. He had to know who Etoile was. Was she Isabelle? And if not, who?

Second and third periods were no better. Isabelle was in fourth-period math class. Jeff wanted to ask her if she was "Etoile." But this email thing was fun. Why ruin it?

And what if he was wrong? What if Isabelle *wasn't* Etoile? He'd make a fool of himself.

As soon as the lunch bell rang, Jeff jumped out of his seat. He ran to the library and logged onto a computer. He smiled when he saw he had an email.

Dear Madscribbler,

I enjoyed meeting your computer alias last night. I feel a bit silly because I don't even know you. But I was thinking about you this morning, so I thought I'd write. I hope you're having fun. I'll be home late tonight—after 9:30. If you want to talk again, that would be great.

Etoile

Jeff's stomach felt like it was in his throat. Either that or he was starving for lunch. He took a deep breath. He tapped his fingers on the keys. Then he started to write.

Dear Etoile,

I had a great time talking to you, too. I did not have a fun morning. English class dragged. So did French, and history, and math. But things got better when I got your email. I'll write again tonight. I have to choke down a peanut butter sandwich and some warm soda before next period. (Maybe I'll sit right next to you and not even realize it.) Talk to you soon.

Madscribbler

Jeff logged off and went to the cafeteria. He sat at an empty table and pulled his lunch out of his backpack.

"Zheff, I have been looking all over for you!" Isabelle sat down next to Jeff. "I tried to talk to you after math class. But you left so quickly. Where were you going?"

Jeff blushed. "Um, I was just hungry, I guess."

"I will not be at the newspaper meeting after school," said Isabelle. "I have to see my parents' friends who are visiting from Paris. They have a son who used to chase me when we were little. He's probably even worse now! But I have to go. I will be home by probably 9:30 or so. Email and tell me what I missed."

Home by 9:30! That was it! Jeff felt his stomach leap into his throat again. But he decided to play it cool. He raised one eyebrow and put on his best smooth voice. "It's funny that you should be sitting right next to me," he said.

Isabelle looked at Jeff. "Why is it funny?" she asked.

"No reason," Jeff said. He tried to keep a straight face. "I guess I'll talk to you later tonight."

❤ ❤ ❤ ❤

At the other end of the cafeteria, Kirsten sat down next to Mike. The first half of the day had dragged for her, too. But now she was feeling much better. She had been thinking about "Madscribbler" all day. After reading his last message, she was sure he *was* sitting right next to her. *Mike and I are such good friends,* she thought. *It's only natural we would like each other on email.*

"So, Kirsten, you look a little tired. Were you up late last night?" asked Mike.

Kirsten smiled. "As if you don't know," she said.

"Huh?" Mike said.

"It's a good thing we stopped for gas the other day. But I wouldn't have gotten upset if we had run out," Kirsten said.

"What are you talking about?" asked Mike.

"You know," Kirsten said. "Done any *mad scribbling* lately?" She poked Mike in the side.

"Ow!" Mike jumped. "What's up with you?"

Kirsten shrugged. She figured that Mike must be joking. Or maybe he was trying to be cool. "Never mind," she said, a little hurt. She tried one last time. "Maybe I'll talk to you tonight?"

"Okay, whatever," said Mike. He started drawing on the corner of his math notebook. Kirsten waited for a moment. Then she gathered her books and left. Mike watched Kirsten walk out of the cafeteria. He made a face, sighed, and went back to drawing.

5

A week later, Kirsten noticed that the new issue of *The Banner* was out.

She grabbed a copy and flipped to the sports section. She looked for the article about the soccer team.

She finally found the article. It was in a tiny corner on the left side of the page. She frowned at the size of the article. Then she started reading.

"*Kristen* Starsia, a halfback on Cleveland High's Varsity Girls' Soccer Team . . ." the article began. *Kristen! Halfback!* Kirsten had corrected Jeff, but he still got it wrong. He made not one, but two big mistakes in the first sentence!

But that wasn't the worst of it. Jeff wrote that the team had *lost* five games. And he also said that the next big game was against the Tigers. (He got *their* name right.) But he said it was an *away* game.

Great job, Jeff, Kirsten thought. *Now nobody will come out to support us!*

♥ ♥ ♥ ♥

Kirsten stormed into the newspaper office. The first person she saw was Tom.

"Is Jeff Kinsley here?" she asked.

Tom pointed to the other side of the room.

Jeff looked up from the articles he was editing. "Hi, Kristen," he said, as she raced toward him.

She waved the paper in his face. "What do you call this!?"

"Um, the latest issue of the paper?" said Jeff.

"Yeah, no kidding! Do you realize that everything you wrote is totally wrong? You screwed everything up!"

"Why don't you tell me how you really feel? No need to be polite," Jeff joked. He stood up and took the newspaper from Kirsten.

Kirsten grabbed the newspaper back and pointed at the article. "You don't seem to care about being correct. Why should I be polite? First of all, my name is *Kirsten,* not *Kristen.* And who told you that we lost five games? We're undefeated! That means we've *never* lost a game!"

Kirsten kept going. "And how could you say that our match against the Tigers is an away game? It's a home game! Now nobody will come watch us!"

She stopped to take a breath. "I guess I should be happy you got the sport right."

"Yeah," said Jeff, trying to be casual. "You play field hockey, right?"

"Funny!" Kirsten yelled. "You wrote that I'm the only player to have scored a goal all season. You make me sound like a conceited jerk! And you didn't even mention that I'm team captain."

"Wait a minute. You're upset that I didn't mention that you're captain. But you think I make you sound conceited?" Jeff raised his eyebrows.

"That is so not the point!" she said.

"Okay, look, I'm sorry about the mistakes." Jeff began to feel bad. "It's not really a big deal. I'll print a correction next week."

Kirsten calmed down. "Well, it's not a *huge* deal. But it *is* important to everyone on the soccer team. Forget the correction, though. The damage is done."

Kirsten crumpled the newspaper into a ball. She dropped it in Jeff's lap and walked out.

"Man, I'd hate to be her boyfriend," Jeff said to Tom. He crumpled the newspaper into an even tighter ball.

"Really?" Tom asked. "I think she's totally cute. Come on, Jeff. You know you messed up. And I know it bothers you. Even if it is *just sports.*"

"It's not a big deal," Jeff said. "I just got some details wrong." He tossed the balled-up newspaper to Tom, who let it fall to the ground.

"Well, here's a little detail for you. Their most important game is next week. If they win, they go to the state championships. No one ever thought they would get that far. It's pretty good for their first season. That's why I wanted to do the piece in the first place. And I know Kirsten wants all the fans to turn out. But you just told the whole school the game is a half-hour away. I'd be mad, too."

Tom left for his math class. Jeff grabbed the crumpled newspaper from the floor. *Ugh! Tom was right. It was pretty bad to have gotten so many facts wrong.* Jeff might not care about sports. But he did care about getting the story right.

Jeff smoothed out the newspaper. Then he noticed the "Perfect Match" ad. Seconds later, his worries were gone. He forgot all about Kirsten. All he could think about was "Etoile."

He glanced over his shoulder. The newspaper office was empty. He went online to see if she had written.

Hey, Madscribbler! It looks like we might get the chance to meet. I can't believe Valentine's Day is so soon. I know it's kind of lame. But I was wondering—are you going to make it to the dance?
   Etoile

Hi, Ms. Star. Good question. We get along so well online . . . should we

really risk meeting?
Madscribbler

Later that night, Kirsten wrote back.

I know what you mean. I'm pretty
freaked out about the whole thing. But
then again, we know we can talk to each
other. So even if there's no chemistry,
we can still be friends, right?
Etoile

I'm glad you said that. Let's just
meet. No pressure or anything.
Madscribbler

Right, no pressure. How about table
six, 9:00? Look for the chick with three
heads. ;)
Etoile

6

What did I say? No pressure? thought Jeff. *Yeah right!* It was only an hour before the dance. He was still tearing through his closet. It was full of jeans and t-shirts. *Since when do I care about what I wear?*

He went to the phone and was about to dial Isabelle. That's who Jeff would normally call. She would calm him down and make him laugh. But how could he call her now? What would he say? "Hey Isabelle, you don't know it. But you have a hot date with me tonight. What do you want me to wear?"

For a second, he pictured her at table six. And he knew what would happen. She would look up at him. Her face would fall. She would try to stop herself. But she'd say out loud, "Oh, no, not you!"

No, no, no. It wouldn't happen that quickly.

It would be long and painful. They wouldn't have anything to say. They'd never be able to work together again. He'd have to quit the newspaper. Maybe he'd talk his parents into moving to Alaska.

Or, on the other hand, suppose it's *not* Isabelle at table six?

❤ ❤ ❤ ❤

Meanwhile, Kirsten was freaking out on the phone with Steph.

"So, are you *nervous*?" teased Steph.

"You are not making this any easier!" Kirsten's voice was faster and louder than usual.

"Oh, come on, just relax. You'll be fine!"

"I know. But I mean, Mike and I have been friends forever. And he has no idea that I'm Etoile. I think he's going to lose it," said Kirsten. *That is, if I don't lose it first,* she thought.

"You and your new *boyfriend* are going to have a great time," said Steph.

"That's enough out of you," Kirsten said. "Listen, I have to get off the phone right now. Or I'll have to show up in my bunny slippers and bathrobe. I need to get dressed. I'll see you later tonight."

Kirsten looked at herself in the mirror. She decided she liked the black pants and green sweater after all. She looked through the pile of clothes on her bed and got dressed. Then she put her hair in a clip and walked out the door.

"That's just great!" Jeff said as he spotted Kirsten entering the gym.

"What's wrong, Jeff?" asked Tom.

"The Soccer Queen's here. Ms. Don't-Get-My-Name-Wrong Starsia. I was hoping to avoid her for the rest of high school."

"She's really not that bad," said Tom. "You just bring out the worst in her."

"I don't know," said Jeff. "I think the worst is all she's got."

"Well, I hope your match shows up soon, Bud," said Tom. "I gotta go find my date. See you later."

Jeff sat down at table six. He didn't want to keep Isabelle waiting. So he had gotten there twenty minutes early. Now he wished he had never shown up at all. Why did Kirsten have to be here? And why was she walking toward him? Jeff looked down and started playing with the table number. He hoped Kirsten would walk by without seeing him.

No such luck. He could tell that she had stopped in front of his table. He refused to look up. But she didn't go away.

He couldn't take it anymore. "Look, if you're here to yell at me, don't. I know I should . . ."

"Right," Kirsten said. "Like I don't have better things to do on a Saturday night than hunt *you* down. I'm sure nobody read your stupid article anyway."

"Yeah, well, it was *such* a great topic," Jeff said. "Remind me. What's the difference between a halfback and a forward center, again?"

"That would be *center forward*," Kirsten said. "You don't learn much from your mistakes, do you?"

"I learned not to do another story on you." Jeff couldn't believe he just said that. He had wanted to say he was sorry. But now he was making everything worse.

"Whatever," Kirsten said. She looked

"Maybe his car broke down," said Jeff.

"What?" asked Kirsten. She turned her head toward him.

"Maybe your match isn't here because his car broke down. That happens. Cars break down. That's the excuse I'm going with. I'll tell everyone, 'Oh, she couldn't make it. Her car broke down.' Do you think they'll buy it?"

Kirsten laughed, "No. But my date is *not* showing up. There's no use sitting here anymore. I'm going to get something to drink." Kirsten stood up. Then she turned to Jeff. "Look, I'm sorry your match didn't show up. Really."

Before Jeff had a chance to answer, Kirsten turned around. She walked quickly to the punch bowl. One of Kirsten's soccer friends ran up to her. Jeff watched as Kirsten talked and laughed.

Jeff was impressed. Kirsten's date hadn't shown up and she didn't seem sour about it. Besides, he thought, she had a great smile.

Why don't we get along, anyway? Jeff wondered, *Is it my fault? Maybe Tom was right.*

Jeff saw Kirsten smile at her friend again. Suddenly, he decided he had to get her to smile like that at him.

Kirsten was standing by herself. Her friend had gone back to her date. Jeff got up and walked over to Kirsten. "Hey, no one claimed either of us. So do you want to dance?" Jeff asked. "Unless you think you'll look more like a loser dancing with me than standing here alone."

Kirsten laughed. She looked at him. "Wait a second," she said. "What position do I play?"

Jeff narrowed his eyes like he was taking a test. "Wide receiver?"

"Right! What's my name?"

"Um, uh, Venus Williams?"

"You didn't even need your notes," said Kirsten, smiling. "Okay, let's dance."

They walked toward the dance floor. Kirsten was glad that she wasn't standing alone anymore. "Thanks," she whispered. But she wasn't sure that he had heard her.

"You're welcome," he whispered back with a grin. "Good idea with the whispering. We wouldn't want anyone to hear us being nice to each other."

Kirsten laughed and they started to dance.

"You're a great dancer, Kirsten. Probably way better than that Ms. Star," said Jeff.

"What do you mean 'Ms. Star'?" asked Kirsten quickly.

"Uh," Jeff was embarrassed. He hadn't meant to say anything about Isabelle. "Well, I was expecting Isabelle, from the paper. She's, um, French. That's how I knew it was her. Her screen name is Etoile. That's French for star."

Kirsten stopped dancing. She looked up at him in shock. "Etoile isn't Isabelle."

"How do you know?" asked Jeff.

"That's not *her* screen name. Etoile . . . star . . . Starsia—get it?" Kirsten stood back. "I can't believe it! *You're* Madscribbler!?"

"Well, I like to write," Jeff said. "I may not always do a great job, but . . ." Jeff looked shocked. "This is so weird," he said.

They stared at each other for half a minute.

Finally, Kirsten smirked. "Does this mean we have to be nice to each other?" she said.

"Do you think we know how?" Jeff asked. The DJ put on something slow. Jeff moved close to Kirsten, and they started to dance again. He could almost feel the warmth of her smile on his shoulder. He smiled, too.

"You know what I still can't believe?" he said.

"What?" her voice was close to his ear.

"*Titanic,*" he said. "How could you possibly think that was a decent movie?"

"Yeah, well, maybe you should work on your interviewing skills," she said. "Then think about becoming a movie critic."

They stopped in the middle of the dance floor. Couples were dancing around them. They looked at each other. Jeff began to smirk. And they started to laugh. People began to stare as they danced by. But Jeff and Kirsten just laughed louder. In a minute, the song ended.

They walked off, their shoulders gently touching. And Jeff turned and whispered, "Maybe you could help me study up on my soccer stats?"